How the
Hibernators
Came to
Bethlehem

Norma Farber

Illustrations by Barbara Cooney

Walker & Company New York

Once upon a winter's night two thousand years ago,
a star shone,
so far, so strong,
it woke every winter-sleeping creature.

Bear was the first to stir.
The heaviest hibernator slept lightest of all.
He only snoozled, really, a kind of cat-nap.
He lay groggy on the north side of a mountain.
In the starlight he looked a great black cushion
such as giants might rest their heads on.

Every hair glistened like patent leather.
The star poked at him with a dainty silver wand,
through fat at least four inches thick.
He stretched and yawned.
The star sang down to him, *Bethlehem*!

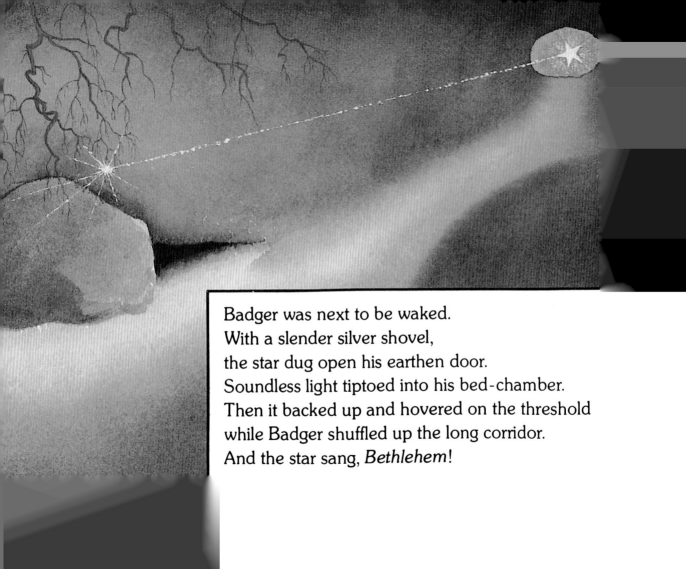

Badger was next to be waked.
With a slender silver shovel,
the star dug open his earthen door.
Soundless light tiptoed into his bed-chamber.
Then it backed up and hovered on the threshold
while Badger shuffled up the long corridor.
And the star sang, *Bethlehem*!

In nearby dens
Skunk and Raccoon were huddled motionless.
The star inserted a silver pass-key,
first at one keyhole, then at the other.
The locks of the hiding-places sprang open.
Skunk and Raccoon shook themselves.
They followed slumbrously where they were led,
as their star sang, *Bethlehem*!

It was Tortoise's turn next.
Starlight flicked open a breathing-space
in the swampy ground near his head.
Slowly, in his heavy suit of armor,
Tortoise pushed himself out of mud and mire
to where the star was singing, *Bethlehem*!

Ground Squirrel, you're next! Wake up!
Oh yes, these dried grasses are soft,
this circular den is cozy,
buried seeds and bulbs so tasty.
But a star has alighted on your lintel,
twirling a wand like a baton.
Time to toddle up the burrow,
to hear how brightly the star sings, *Bethlehem*!

And now the star hovered over Bat
as he turned rightside up under the eave
where he had been hanging upside down.
For he had been resting only fitfully.
A breath of fresh air, he thought,
should help me fall asleep.

A silver feather tapped him between the eyes.
He sneezed so loud the star twinkled.
He stretched his full length,
and spread out his full breadth,
alert and curious to hear the star sing, *Bethlehem*!
Follow me to Bethlehem!

In short order
the star sang every winter-sleeping creature awake—
 Bird,
          Mammal,
                    Reptile,
                              Amphibian,
                                        Fish,
                                             Insect.

The Polka-dotted Ladybird,
the Black and Yellow Spider,
even the Garden Snail.

One and all, they proceeded,
a great night-caravan, where the song led.
And the star sang them all the way to Bethlehem.

In no time at all they came to a manger.
There Lion and Lamb and dozens of other animals
were already gathered close.
They were watching a newborn baby in a mound of sweet hay.

Three Kings were there also,
kneeling.
"Look!" said the Kings.
"Even the hibernators have come!"

And everyone was very quiet, listening, while the star sang on and on, *Bethlehem*!

And on and on and on, *Bethlehem*!

This story was written for Helen Margaret by Norma Farber.

These pictures were drawn for Sammy by Granny.

Text copyright © 1966 by Norma Farber
Illustrations copyright © 1980 by Barbara Cooney

First published in the United States of America in 1980 by
Walker Publishing Company, Inc.
This edition published 2006
Distributed to the trade by Holtzbrinck Publishers

For information about permission to reproduce selections from
this book, write to Permissions, Walker & Company,
104 Fifth Avenue, New York, New York 10011

Library of Congress Cataloging-in-Publication Data cataloged the original edition as follows:
Farber, Norma.
How the hibernators came to Bethlehem.
Summary: The Star of Bethlehem awakens the winter-sleeping creatures, such as Bear, Badger, and Racoon, to send them to visit a new born baby.
[1. Christmas stories] I. Cooney, Barbara. II. Title.
PZ7.F2228Ho 1980   [E]   80-7685

ISBN-10: 0-8027-9610-9 • ISBN-13: 978-0-8027-9610-3 (hardcover)
ISBN-10: 0-8027-9611-7 • ISBN-13: 978-0-8027-9611-0 (reinforced)

Visit Walker & Company's Web site at www.walkeryoungreaders.com

Printed in China

2 4 6 8 10 9 7 5 3 1

All papers used by Walker & Company are natural, recyclable products
made from wood grown in well-managed forests. The manufacturing processes
conform to the environmental regulations of the country of origin.